Snow White

Maggie Moore and The Pope Twins

W
FRANKLIN WATTS
LONDON•SYDNEY

Chapter 1:
A Beautiful Princess

Once upon a time there was a
beautiful and kind-hearted princess
called Snow White.

She lived in the royal palace with her
stepmother, the queen. The queen was
beautiful, but very vain and very jealous.
She wanted to be the most beautiful
woman in the land.

Every day she asked her magic mirror:
"Mirror, mirror on the wall,
who's the fairest of them all?"

Every time the mirror replied:
"I have searched and I understand
that you are the fairest in the land."
The queen was always very pleased.

Chapter 2:
The Jealous Queen

As Snow White grew older, she grew more and more beautiful. Everyone loved her because she was so kind and everyone admired her beauty.

One day, when the queen asked her magic mirror who was the fairest in the land, she had a horrible surprise.

The mirror told her:
"Beautiful queen, though you're still grand,
Snow White is now the fairest in the land."

The jealous queen was furious. She hated
Snow White. She commanded a huntsman
to be brought to the palace.

"Go," she ordered him. "Take Snow White
into the forest and kill her with this dagger.
Bring back her heart as proof."

The huntsman was horrified. He took Snow White into the forest, but said to her, "Run for your life, away from the wicked queen. I will take her the heart of an animal so she thinks that you are dead. Go quickly."

Snow White thanked the huntsman and ran deep into the forest until, at last, she found a little house. It had seven little beds and seven little chairs. It was the home of seven dwarfs and it looked warm and inviting.

The dwarfs were surprised to see her, but Snow White said she would look after their house while they worked. She also cooked their food so they were all very happy. They wanted her to stay, because she was so kind.

Chapter 3:
The Queen's Disguises

Meanwhile the wicked queen was so sure that Snow White was dead that she had stopped asking her magic mirror the question. However, one day, she decided to check that she was still the fairest.

The mirror replied:
"Beautiful queen, though you're still grand, Snow White is STILL the fairest in the land."

"What!" the queen cried. "That huntsman has tricked me." She stormed around in a rage and commanded her spies to find Snow White.

Eventually the queen found out where Snow White was hiding. She realised that nobody else would want to kill her, so she decided to do the awful deed herself.

She disguised herself as an old ribbon seller
and went to the little house.

"Please buy my ribbons," she said. "I am
poor and hungry."

Snow White felt sorry for the old woman.
"Come inside," she said, "and rest for a
while. You must be tired."

The queen offered to show Snow White how
to wear the ribbons. She tied them so tightly
around her waist that Snow White could not
breathe and she fell unconscious to the floor.

18

Luckily, the dwarfs arrived home in
time to save her. They saw what was
wrong and quickly untied the ribbons.
"Do not let anyone else into the
house," they told her. "The wicked queen
is trying to kill you."

At the palace, the queen's magic mirror told her that Snow White was still alive.

She disguised herself again and took a poisoned comb to the house. Snow White opened the door, but would not let her in. "Just let me show you," said the queen, and she pushed the comb through Snow White's hair right into her scalp. Snow White staggered and fell against the door.

When the dwarfs returned they saw the comb sticking in her head and quickly pulled it out.

"Do not even open the door to anyone. Another time we could be too late to save you," they warned.

Once more the mirror told the queen that Snow White was still alive. So the queen prepared a poisoned apple and disguised herself as an apple seller. Again she went to the little house.

"Taste my apple," she said to Snow White. Snow White remembered the dwarfs' warning and refused it. The queen craftily bit into one half to show it was safe, and offered the other half to Snow White. But that other half was poisoned. Snow White bit into it and collapsed onto the floor. The queen yelled with joy and ran off.

Chapter 4:
The Glass Case

This time the dwarfs were too late to save Snow White. They could not see what was wrong with her. Eventually, they built a beautiful glass case and put her gently into it. They sat by her to protect her.

Nearby, a prince was out hunting with his men and saw the weeping dwarfs and the glass case. He went up to them to see what was wrong and saw Snow White. He thought she was the most beautiful girl he had ever seen.

"You cannot leave her here," he said to the dwarfs. "She should be in a palace. Come with me all of you. We will all protect her." He ordered his men to lift the glass case.

As the prince's men lifted the case, one of them stumbled. The case wobbled and the poisoned apple fell from Snow White's mouth. She opened her eyes and saw the prince. The dwarfs were overjoyed and danced with happiness. The prince's huntsmen smiled and cheered.

Chapter 5:
A Royal Wedding

The prince lifted Snow White to her feet.
Snow White and the prince did not notice
the dwarfs dancing or the huntsmen
cheering because they had fallen in love!

Snow White and the prince were kind and invited the wicked queen to their wedding. But the magic mirror had again told her that Snow White was the fairest in the land. She was so angry that she smashed the magic mirror – and she was never seen again!

About the story

Snow White is a German fairy tale, first published by the Brothers Grimm in their collection of stories in 1812. It is now one of the best known fairy tales in the world. In their first version, it is Snow White's mother, not stepmother, who is the villain. Some people think that the story is based on a real person called Maria Sophia von Erthal, born in 1729. She was a kind girl with an evil stepmother who poisoned her with an apple and even owned a talking mirror! Talking mirrors were very popular at the time and could repeat words you said to them. Variations of the story have been traced around the world, from India to Albania.

Be in the story!

Imagine you are the stepmother. What might you be thinking when you receive an invitation to Snow White's wedding?

Now imagine you are Snow White. Write a letter to the huntsman describing your time at the dwarfs' house and being woken up by the prince!

First published in 2014 by
Franklin Watts
338 Euston Road
London
NW1 3BH

Franklin Watts Australia
Level 17/207 Kent Street
Sydney
NSW 2000

A CIP catalogue record for this book is available
from the British Library.

The artwork for this story first appeared in
Hopscotch Fairy Tales: Snow White

ISBN 978 1 4451 3009 5 (hbk)
ISBN 978 1 4451 3010 1 (pbk)
ISBN 978 1 4451 3012 5 (library ebook)
ISBN 978 1 4451 3011 8 (ebook)

Series Editor: Jackie Hamley
Series Advisor: Catherine Glavina
Series Designer: Cathryn Gilbert

Printed in China

Franklin Watts is a divison of
Hachette Children's Books,
an Hachette UK company.
www.hachette.co.uk